To my mom, Lylia,
who created this story with me
and made me hiccup from laughter while doing so.

www.enchantedlion.com

First edition, published in 2019 by Enchanted Lion Books,
67 West Street, Studio 317A, Brooklyn, NY 11222
Text and Illustrations copyright © 2019 by Masha Manapov
Production & Graphic Design: Eugenia Mello
All rights reserved under International and Pan-American Copyright Conventions
A CIP record is on file with the Library of Congress. ISBN 978-1-59270-300-5
Printed in China by RR Donnelley Asia Printing Solutions Ltd.
1 3 5 7 9 10 8 6 4 2

ARIBA

AN OLD TALE ABOUT NEW SHOES

Based on a story that has traveled around the world

MASHA MANAPOV

ENCHANTED LION BOOKS
NEW YORK

From the moment Marcus put on his new shoes,
he couldn't stop moving. He bounced all the way
from the living room to the kitchen, circled
the house 3 times and the shed 3 times more,
climbed the tree in Billy's backyard,

ran up

and

down the 19 steps to his front door,
and accidentally stepped on Carlos' tail.

He even jumped so high that he almost reached his
father's nose! And there's no doubt that his father
is the tallest in the family by far.

Marcus' new shoes lit up and flashed in two colors.
If his mother would only let him, he would wear
them to bed.

There wasn't a single person to whom Marcus
didn't present his new shoes. He showed them
off to Billy's mother, the bus driver, the ice cream
man, Mr. Samson and his annoying little dog
from across the street, and just about everyone
else who happened to cross his path.

Just as he was running out of people to appreciate his shoes, his grandfather called. Grandpa listened closely to everything Marcus had to say, then asked him, "How do you feel in your shoes?"

"I feel great!" Marcus said.
        "I can bounce, roll, and jump super high. Like a superhero!"

"Ah, yes," Grandpa replied after a short pause. "This reminds me of a story that happened a long time ago. Would you like to hear it?" Marcus snuggled deep into his chair. He loved Grandpa's stories.

Under an endless sky, in a small village surrounded by high mountains, there once lived a boy named Ariba. During the day, he herded sheep, and as the long evenings darkened into night, he gazed up at the stars.

For his twelfth birthday, his parents gave him a pair of shoes.
Not old shoes or hand-me-downs, but brand new shoes. They
were sturdy and, oh boy, were they big. So big that Ariba
would be able to wear them for a long, long time. After all,
feet grow very fast.

"These shoes will never wear out," his mother said proudly.

At first, Ariba couldn't take his eyes off them. He hugged them for a very long minute. Then, overjoyed, he threw them up into the air, caught one in each hand, and walked around with his feet high in the sky.

Ariba decided he would wear his shoes
only on Sundays and very special occasions.
During the week, they lay on on the mat
by the door, waiting. As it turned out,
his shoes loved adventures.

Once they took him to the highest peak of the yellow mountain.
On another occasion, they helped put out a fire in the yard.
I've heard they even led him to track down the village robber.
And then there was that funny night when they urged him
        to dance at a wedding...

Growing up with them was never boring.
Even on days when they did nothing particularly
unusual together and simply gazed up at the sky.

As time went by, Ariba's friends began to leave
the village for the city. At first, Ariba wanted to
stay. But then he got to wondering what the sky
was like over there, beyond the high mountains.

And so one morning, he put on his shoes and went
on his way, taking the rugged road.

When Ariba arrived in the city, there was so much to see.
But the sky had become very small, and the stars seemed
to have completely disappeared.

Soon he forgot to ever look up.

For his new home,
Ariba bought
a new bed,

a new table,

a new chair,

and a new pair of shoes.

His old ones didn't seem to fit his
new life, so he carefully cleaned
them up and put them outside.

Not long afterwards, some children spotted the shoes and recognized them at once.

"These are our new neighbor's shoes! He was wearing them when he arrived. Let's leave them by his door."

How surprised Ariba was when he opened the door!

"Well, old friends," he said, "I see you missed me. But how on earth did you return, and what are you doing here? You know I don't have time for games, like I used to."

This time Ariba decided that he would discard his shoes at the train station.

Surely, someone will find them and take them far away, he thought.

But the very same day, the Inspector who knew everything and everyone was patrolling the train station.

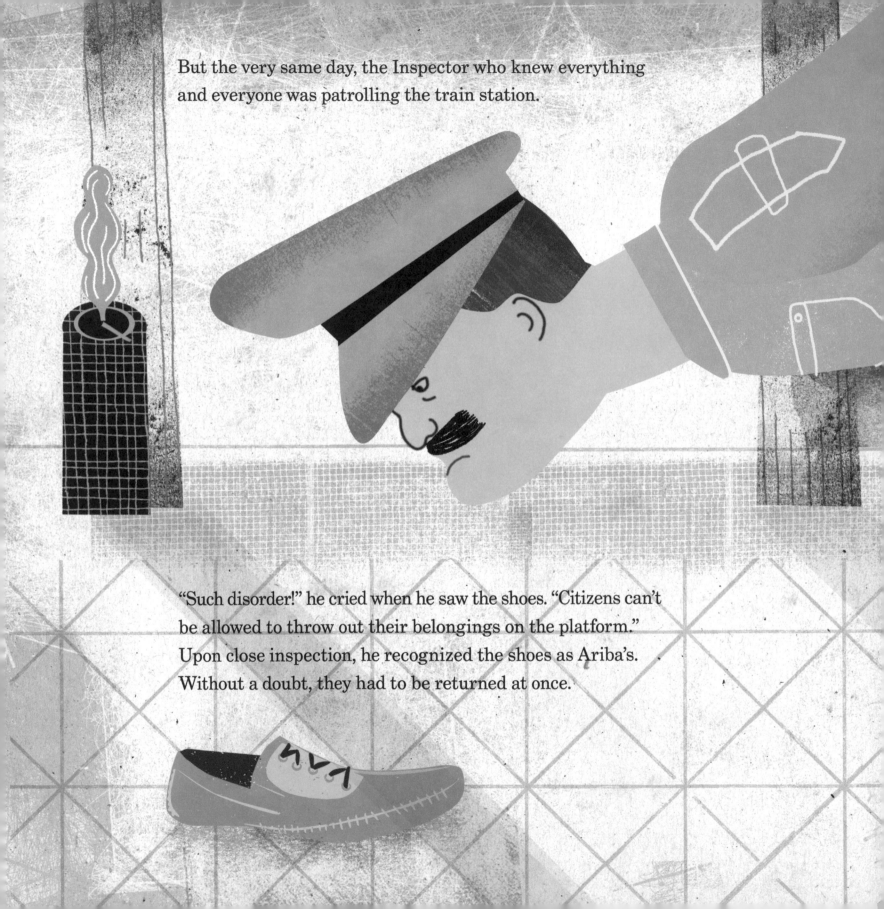

"Such disorder!" he cried when he saw the shoes. "Citizens can't be allowed to throw out their belongings on the platform." Upon close inspection, he recognized the shoes as Ariba's. Without a doubt, they had to be returned at once.

When Ariba got home from work and found the shoes
back on his doorstep, he looked around, rubbing his
eyes in astonishment.

"How could you have possibly gotten back here?"
Ariba exclaimed. "And why won't you leave me be?
I have no use for you anymore."

This time he decided to take them far beyond the street,
the park, and even the train station.

There's no way they'll find their way back now! he thought.

But a few days later, as the story goes,
a woman spotted the shoes and picked them up.

She asked around until someone said, "I know
who these belong to! They are Ariba's shoes.
We grew up together in the village. He was very
fond of them and wore them every Sunday.
We should return them to him."

40 44 49

41 45 50

42 46 51

43 47 52

This time, when Ariba saw his old shoes,
he was struck by a realization and said,
"You know what, I am truly happy to see you.
Let's never leave each other again."

That same night, Ariba put on his old shoes. They led him to the darkest spot in the city, where once again he looked up and finally saw the starry sky.

"What a journey those shoes have been on," Marcus said, having listened and laughed along with the whole story.

"I'm so happy they came back. After all, I really like being with you on Sundays. We always have the most fantastic time together."